The Children of the
MORNING LIGHT

The Children of the
MORNING LIGHT

WAMPANOAG TALES
as Told by Manitonquat (Medicine Story)
illustrated by Mary F. Arquette

Macmillan Publishing Company   New York
Maxwell Macmillan Canada   Toronto
Maxwell Macmillan International   New York   Oxford   Singapore   Sydney

1   3   5   7   9   10   8   6   4   2

Library of Congress Cataloging-in-Publication Data
Medicine Story. The Children of the Morning Light : Wampanoag tales as told by Manitonquat (Medicine Story) / illustrated by Mary F. Arquette. — 1st ed.   p.   cm. Summary: A collection of traditional stories that describe the creation of the world and the early history of the Wampanoag Indians in southeastern Massachusetts. ISBN 0-02-765905-4   1. Wampanoag Indians—Legends. 2. Wampanoag Indians—Religion and mythology—Juvenile literature. [1. Wampanoag Indians— Legends.   2. Wampanoag Indians—Religion and mythology.   3. Indians of North America—Massa- chusetts—Legends.   4. Indians of North America—Massachusetts—Religion and mythology. 5. Creation—Folklore.]   I. Arquette, Mary F., ill.   II. Title.
E99.W2M43   1994   398.2'089973—dc20   92-32328

To the memory of my mother,
Priscilla Gov Affeld, 1908–93,
who introduced me to the world's literature,
encouraged my writing,
and whose praise at last was my greatest reward.
—MANITONQUAT

To my father, Francis Arquette
—M. F. A.

CONTENTS

AUTHOR'S NOTE

These stories are from the oral traditions of the Pokonoket or mainland Wampanoag of southeastern Massachusetts. Although a few of them bear similarities to stories of other peoples, most are totally unique and not to be found in any other source. I have been telling these stories at our traditional ceremonies for many years, and I am proud of what they reveal of the strength of the culture of our people.

That is one reason why I take the step to commit them to print for the first time, a step I have considered long and seriously. Something different happens when a story is put into print. It is frozen there, no longer with the same life given it each time by each storyteller. On the other hand, many more people can benefit from the wisdom of these old tales, and many more children can learn about our people and how we understand the world.

It is to my grandfather that I owe all my appreciation for having the patience to tell me these stories, and many more, again and again so that I could remember and pass them along to my children, and to him I owe apologies for any lapses in my memory, anything I may have distorted or left out. I am also grateful that these stories will not only be frozen in this volume, but that my two sons know and tell them, so they will stay alive for the future generations of our people.

—Manitonquat

THE MORNING
OF THE WORLD

The Old Storyteller stirs up the coals and puts a few more sticks on the fire. Everyone is quiet, for they know a story is coming. His voice, when it comes at last, is quiet, but clear, and seems to reach with the flickering light into the shadows. Listen.

Gather around me closely now, close to one another, my dear ones, and keep each other warm while I tell you of the Song of Creation.

THE SONG OF CREATION

We are known as the People of the Dawn, the Wampanoag, Children of the Morning Light. This is a story we have of the beginnings of things.

At first there was nothing. Only Kiehtan was there, our people say, that Great Mystery whose name is also Kishtannit, the Big Spirit. There in the nothing Kiehtan began to sing, and there was joy in his song. Time began. The song was the Song of Creation, and the singer, Kiehtan, sang up time and then sang up space and then sang up movement to dance through the space.

Pretty soon Kiehtan, the Creator, thought it would be good to have something to dance with this energy, so from it he began to sing up some substance. Then Kiehtan sang up some star makers to go out and gather together the clouds of this mass. They brought these clouds together so tightly that they became hot and began to burn. Here and there in the far distances of space, fires began to burn in the dark, and these became the stars. These the starmakers put together in star nations, star tribes, star clans, and star families. We can see some of them now at night, wandering on their sacred roads through the heavens, still dancing in their circles.

Kiehtan the Creator saw that all the starmakers had different thoughts. The singer thought this was good, for now the new universe would have many kinds of ideas. All possible thoughts would be available for the Song of Creation.

One of the starmakers we call Hobomoko. Each of the starmakers had a different way of thinking, and Hobomoko's special way of thinking was like this: He thought that everything was wrong. He thought that Kiehtan the Creator was making mistakes everywhere.

Hobomoko was the kind who is always complaining. Nothing is right, he thought. It is all dangerous and untrustworthy. He tried to warn the other starmakers and tell them how bad everything was, but they did not think that way, of course, and so they did not believe him.

This Hobomoko is the one who made the fire we call our sun, Nepaushet. Today we call Nepaushet "Grandfather," because he is elder to all our relatives here, but in that early morning of Creation when he was young, he was alone. He felt lonely because the other star fires were far away, and he danced all by himself about his great fire and sang his song all alone.

Then Nepaushet heard another song, a pretty song coming from somewhere below him. He looked down and saw two lovely sisters dancing together and singing so sweetly. These sisters were Nanepaushet and Paumpagusset, spirits of the moon and the ocean. We call them "Grandmother" today, but at that time they were very young and even then very beautiful, and they had only each other. Paumpagusset was dark and mysterious, and her dance rose and fell in a turbulent rhythm. Nanepaushet was bright and serene, and her dance moved slowly around her sister. There was joy and much love in the song they sang and the dance they danced together.

When Grandfather Sun saw the dance and heard the song of these sisters, he began to love them. He was glad not to be alone, and he did not want them to leave, so he said to them, "Sisters, I would like you to stay with me. Perhaps one of you would marry me, but I cannot choose between you because you are both so beautiful."

And the sisters answered, "We like you well enough, but we love each other so much that we cannot part from each other. Therefore if you will marry both of us, we will stay and be your wives."

And so Grandmother Ocean came gladly to live in the lodge of Grandfather Sun, and with her shyly and silently came Grandmother Moon. The two sisters lived and danced and sang around the warm fire of Grandfather Sun, and they loved him, each in her own way. And so they sing and dance together still the Dance of the Grandmothers, the dance of all women.

Nanepaushet, the moon, bathed in the light of Nepaushet, the sun, and gave it back to the dancing waters of Paumpagusset, the ocean. But Paumpagusset drew Nepaushet's power into her and kept it. The energy of Nepaushet sang in the depths of the ocean, and seeds began to grow there.

From this song Keesaqu't, the sky, was conceived and was born. Father Sky embraced his mother Paumpagusset and reached toward his father, Nepaushet. And then Metta'oky, Mother Earth, was conceived and began to grow, deep in the womb of Grandmother Ocean.

SKY WOMAN AND THE TWINS

A bove, beyond the clouds and the blue robe of Father Sky, there were many stars and lights and worlds, but below was only water—for Mother Earth had not yet been born—a great, vast, dark ocean, and the sky full of light, bright and turquoise and shining all over. And in the middle of the sky there was one being who kept a tree full of lights. That was his responsibility, that particular sky spirit.

And there was another sky spirit, a female spirit, a daughter of Morning Star and Grandmother Moon, and this young sky woman had a dream that the West Wind was going to make her pregnant. This dream upset her because she had never met the West Wind, and she didn't like to think that her life was going to be toyed with like that. It frightened her. So she went to the wise person who was the caretaker of the sacred tree of lights and told him about the dream. Well, immediately he saw that the dream was going to come true, but he didn't want to frighten her more, so he said he would protect her.

She said, "Oh, hide me. Hide me from him."

So he said, "All right. I'll pull up the tree here. You climb into the hole underneath."

So she did—and she began to fall through the hole, and she came slowly down through the sky toward the ocean. And of course during that long, long fall, the West Wind found her and

loved her and sang to her and danced with her, and, well, by the time she reached the ocean, she was pregnant.

The spirit of Great Turtle looked up from inside the ocean and sent up some spirits to bring her gently to rest on his back, and then they went back down where all the dark spirits of the ocean were.

And what was growing in her womb were twins who became known as Maushop and Matahdou. Now Maushop was to be the firstborn by his position in the womb. But Hobomoko came to the other one, Matahdou, and whispered to him even in the womb. He said, "You know, the Creation is not working out right. The Creator's making mistakes—and look at you! You're placed to be second-born here and Maushop is going to be firstborn, and that doesn't feel right."

And Matahdou said, "No. It doesn't feel right at all." He said, "Brother, move out of the way. I should be born first."

And Maushop said, "No, the Creator put me here, so this is where I'm supposed to be born. And the Creator put you there, so you're supposed to come second."

And they had a big argument right there, inside their mother's belly, and what finally happened was that Maushop wouldn't give way, because he said Matahdou should be content at the way Creation is and Creation is all right. And Matahdou was already upset.

While Maushop was being born the right way, Matahdou burst out through the side and killed his mother. Well, I don't know how you kill a sky spirit, but I guess that'll do it. And from then on, they were raised by their grandmother, the moon.

MAUSHOP BUILDS
TURTLE ISLAND

As Maushop and Matahdou were growing up, eventually they had the responsibility for creating things, for helping the Creator on this world. There were many other spirits. They say that those sea spirits lived in villages and great cities under the ocean, and that they all lived very happily under the water there.

So at first Maushop and Matahdou began to make things in the water. They made little plants and little fish, and they got fancier and fancier with it. They made really good things. They made water birds, like geese and heron, and water animals, too. And then later on they went up on top of Great Turtle, and they wanted to make things there, too. The fish told them Mother Earth was down below in the womb of the ocean, so the diving birds went down to look. The tern and the duck couldn't see anything, but the loon went much farther and said, "Yes, there is earth there, but I could not go that far."

So Maushop asked the sea animals that he and his brother had been making, and the beaver said that he was a good swimmer, so he would try to bring up some earth. After a while he came back exhausted and said he couldn't make it. Then the otter said, "I'm a better swimmer than you; I'll go," but he couldn't get that far down, either.

Then the little muskrat offered to go, and the other animals laughed because he was so small. But the little muskrat had a lot of heart, and he went down and was gone for a long, long time, until they all thought he must be dead.

Then suddenly his little nose came up out of the ocean, and he was unconscious. They dragged him out of the water, and they found there was a little bit of mud on the end of his nose.

So Maushop took that little piece of mud and began to roll it between his hands, and it got bigger and bigger. Then he took the ball of mud and rolled it out on the shell of the turtle, and it grew and grew, and he spread it all over.

Maushop made a great island on the turtle's back, and that is this land where we live now. Then he and Matahdou made more islands and they began to create more creatures on these islands.

There was one thing about their creating, though: Matahdou always tried to imitate what his brother did, but because his mind was continually filled with jealousy, the things he did weren't so good.

Maushop would make some beautiful little fish, and Matahdou would go next and he'd create poisonous jellyfish or barracudas or sea monsters or something like that. And when they got to creating things on the land, Maushop would create pretty little herbs and helpful healing things and trees and flowers and vegetables. Matahdou would start creating and he'd create poison ivy and poison oak, poison mushrooms, and those kinds of things. They had his anger in them.

Maushop would create pretty little butterflies and nice hummingbirds and dragonflies and all these beautiful things that delight us. And Matahdou would create blackflies and mosquitoes and hornets and wasps and red ants. So anything that you can't see any possible use for in Creation, well, you can blame them on poor old Matahdou. He was trying his best, but his mind was all clouded up with jealousy, and he didn't do so well. He made many huge monsters on the land, and monster birds, too, that later Maushop had to subdue or make smaller.

For instance, the squirrel was once as big as a tall tree and he was always smashing things with his huge tail. But Maushop began to pet him, smoothing his hand over his back and tail, and Squirrel began to get smaller and smaller until he got down to the size he is today. Beaver was also a monster once, and he tried to get away from Maushop, and before Maushop caught up with him to bring him down to his present size, he had made the Great Lakes. Moose is pretty big, but once he was even bigger. He tried to run away, too, but Maushop stood in front of him and held up his hand. Moose was going so fast that he couldn't stop and he ran right into Maushop's hand, which is why today the moose still has a pushed-in nose and a humped back.

After a while, Maushop and Matahdou had just stuffed the world with many different islands and many different kinds of vegetation and many different kinds of animals and birds and everything you can think of. Now it came time for human beings to be created. So Maushop thought, First we have to have a new kind of body for this human-being spirit to get into.

So he went to a particular island and he found clay cliffs that had four different kinds of clay in them, red and white and black and yellow. When you mix those four colors you get brown, and that was the color of the bodies Maushop made for

these new people. Some he mixed a little more black so that they would be darker brown, some he mixed with more white so that they would be lighter skinned, and with more red or more yellow they were more ruddy or more olive. Those four colors are our sacred colors, and each of the four directions has a color, white for north, yellow for east, red for south, and black for west.

And those clays, which you can see today, are in the area we call Aquinah, which is Gay Head on the island of Martha's Vineyard. It has big cliffs made of those four colors of clay.

And Maushop went out and he carved a face, a head, out of a living tree, and he used such a head for each of these beings. Then he thought, Well, they need more than just these bodies to move around with. They need some things that maybe some of the other animals don't have as much of. They need to get a little bit more. So first let's give them really good minds so that they will know how to build their houses and canoes, make their clothes, and survive well in this world. And then let's give them hearts with good feelings so that they'll be able to know love and joy and beauty, and that will guide them in their lives, however they want to be. They can follow their hearts—see what is beautiful and loving and true.

And then the final thing was, he took some of the Spirit of Creation and breathed that into them so that they would always know they were part of the great Song of Creation. Maushop taught them that they could follow their original instructions, like every other being; just as a squirrel was always a squirrel because he was following his instructions, so human beings could learn how to be human beings in the world.

FIRSTMAN

The first man-being that Maushop made we call Firstman. On the first morning of his life he was alone in this new world and wondering what he was supposed to do there. Of course he didn't understand yet what everything was for and how things worked, and there were no other people to talk to, so he just walked around and looked at things and wondered about them.

Then he saw Maushop, who was busy making something new. Firstman went up to Maushop and said, "Do you know what goes on in this place? I am new here myself, and I don't know what I am supposed to do. There's no one to talk to, so I don't even know who I am."

Maushop looked up and said, "Oh, Firstman, there you are. Yes, of course, you don't know anything yet. But I don't have time to talk right now. I am very busy trying to get the design right on this butterfly wing. Why don't you go ask your grandmother?"

"My grandmother? I didn't know I had a grandmother!" Firstman exclaimed. In fact, he didn't really know what a grandmother was, but as soon as he heard that he had one, he loved her. His heart just filled right up with love for his grandmother (because all people love their grandmothers, don't

they?), and he knew right away that he had to go and see her. "Oh, yes, I want to see my grandmother! Where is she?"

"Well, she lives in that lodge just across the river there."

"Thank you." Firstman started to go, then came back. "Just one more thing, if I could ask. What is a river?"

"Well, when you run down that hill, you will find it. Just go across, and the lodge will be right there."

Firstman was so excited that he ran down the hill and tried to run right across the river. Of course, he had never seen water before, and he didn't know that it wasn't solid like the ground. So he sank down, and the current of the river swept him off his feet and dumped him back on the shore again.

That's funny stuff, Firstman thought. It's too soft to walk on. Maybe I'll take some of this hard earth and throw it in to make a path across. But the river just took all the dirt he threw in it and washed it away.

Then he tried to roll big rocks into the river, but they sank all the way to the bottom.

Firstman sat down on the bank and began to think. He now noticed that there were stones and pebbles under the water, but that leaves and twigs drifted on top of it.

So some things sink and some things float, he thought. Pretty soon he saw a big branch of a tree come floating down the river, and a bird was sitting on it, getting a ride.

Ah-ha, he rides on that log and floats, thought Firstman. Maybe I could do that, too. So he looked around in the woods and found a big log and dragged it to the river and sat on it in the water. It sank under his weight, but he could feel it pushing up on him, so he thought that perhaps since he was bigger than the bird, he would need two logs. When he got another log and sat on both of them together, they also sank, but he could feel that they were a little stronger.

Well, if two are better than one, then three will be better than two, and—well, I'll get a lot of them. But when he had several of them in the water, they would not stay together.

He looked around. Hanging down from a tree was a long vine. He pulled it down and wrapped the vine around all the logs and tied them together. Now when he stood on them, they held him up. All he had to figure out was how to make them all go across the river.

He found a pole and began to push with it while he stood on the logs. They started to move, and in a little while he had pushed them all the way across to the other side of the river. Sure enough, there was his grandmother's lodge right nearby.

"Come in, Grandson! Sit down, catch your breath and rest, have a little corn soup, and tell me all about your day."

Firstman was so excited about all that had happened to him on his first day, and how he had solved the problem of getting across the river, that he just talked and talked and told her everything.

Then he said, "But, Grandmother, Maushop told me that I should ask you about what I am supposed to do in the world. Can you tell me?"

She said, "You have just had your first lesson. Your heart told you to come and speak to me, and your mind showed you how to cross the river, and that's the lesson. Always follow your heart. When you want to know what to do, ask your heart. And when you want to know how to do it, use your mind. Always use your mind to show you how to follow the direction of your heart, but never the other way around. Your mind can learn, and it knows what it learns, but only the heart knows love and beauty, and they are the Creator's guides."

STORY OF THE SWEAT LODGE

So Maushop had given those four gifts to the human beings: the gift of the body made from the clay, the gift of the mind protected by the skull carved from the living trees, the gift of the heart to give them the guides of love and beauty and joy, and the Creator's spirit to make them related to all Creation.

Now Matahdou decided that he'd better give some gifts to these human beings, too, so he called everybody together for a big giveaway and he presented four gifts to everybody. Everybody had to take them because it was a great honor to have a giveaway, but when they found out what they were, they were very upset. They were really four poisons. He gave a poison to their bodies, which was disease. They had never been sick before that. And he gave a poison to their minds, which was confusion, so they no longer always knew what was true. He gave them a poison to their hearts, fear, which created all kinds of other bad feelings. And last of all he gave a poison to the spirit. Of course, the spirit is part of the Creator and you can't really hurt it, but what he gave them was a sort of forgetfulness so that they forgot that they had that spirit and that they were part of the one family of Creation—that there was only one spirit in the world and that they were all part of it and were all related to everything.

So Maushop got very angry with his brother—for the first

time. And they began to have a big fight. They began wrestling and throwing each other and jumping around all over the universe, hurling stars at each other, breaking up everything that was around them. And the fight got bigger and bigger, because the both of them were evenly matched, and neither one of them could defeat the other one.

And the spirits of the four directions watched this go on and they began to get upset, saying, "These fellows are going to destroy the whole universe before it's time. We've got a whole lot of years to go in this universe, and they're going to destroy it right now. We're going to have to do something."

So they said, "We're going to leave Maushop down there on Metta'oky, the earth, because he is a friend of all those creatures there and he's good for them, and we'll send Matahdou off to some other place."

So they did. They told Maushop to throw his brother into the flames of the big fire. He did, and his brother went up in smoke. As he was going off in smoke, Matahdou said to his brother, "I'm going off to this other place and I'll come back in a few days and tell you about what it's like."

Maushop sat there after Matahdou was gone and said, "Well, that's all very well. That takes care of Matahdou, I guess. But what about these poor human beings who have all these sicknesses now?"

He thought about it and he thought about it, and the fire went down. He wasn't getting anywhere. The kids were all running underfoot, and the dogs were barking, and everybody was making too much noise, so he said, "I'll go back into my cave and meditate."

So he went and closed himself in the dark and he sat there in the quiet and he thought and he thought. And he got kind of cold. That's about all he got. So he went out to the fire and he got a few rocks that had been in the fire and were glowing red-hot and he brought them into the cave with him and closed it with a bearskin again and sat there. And the rocks glowed and the whole cave got hot. It got very hot. He began to perspire. So he took a little skin of water and he had a drink and as he did, it spilled onto the rocks and it went *hiss-ss-ss-ss*—and steam hit him in the face. And he had an inspiration, a vision, right there. "Ah, this is the way human beings can heal themselves!"

So he went out and he gathered everybody around and he said, "Now listen, everybody. This is what we've got to do with these poisons that you've got now. Whenever you get yourself sick, you've got to build a fire. The fire is the force that runs throughout the universe. It's the stars. It's the sun. It's everything that moves. It's that energy that's in there.

"And in that fire you put some rocks. They represent all the things in our universe—all the human beings, all the animals, the earth, everything that there is. And they sit in the fire and they get filled with this energy.

"Then you take them into a little cave, or you make a little lodge and you bring the rocks and some water in with you. And you close yourself in there and you make it all dark. What you've done is you've created a small universe. And in that universe you have everything in the big universe with you, all infused with the energy.

"And you take some water. The water spirit is the spirit of life. You pour that on those rocks and the spirit of the air and the winds will bring the healing power that takes place there, all through your bodies, and make you sweat. You'll breathe it into you and it'll go through your blood. And it'll purify you.

"And if at the same time you sing some songs, shake a little rattle or something, you'll be putting everything into harmony inside your little universe, you see, because when you're sick, you're out of harmony or out of rhythm with the rhythm of the universe, so you put it all back together again."

And that is how we got the sweat lodge, which our people still use to heal and purify themselves, or to find a vision or wisdom to guide their lives.

HOW DEATH CAME
INTO THE WORLD

After that Maushop was sitting by the fire late at night as the moon started to rise through the woods. Suddenly the frogs stopped singing, and he looked up to see what was the matter. There was Matahdou coming back in the moonlight, but he didn't seem all there. It was like he was made of smoke, and part of him was missing.

Maushop called out, "Brother, I don't think you are supposed to be here. You have left some of yourself somewhere else!"

Matahdou was sad as he spoke. "Brother, it is very lonely where I am now. The healing powers have made me the keeper of the door of the land of souls, but there is no one there, and I am all alone."

Maushop said, "I guess it is time for us to consider the question of death in the world. We will have a council here, but you should go back to that other place now."

So Maushop called everyone together. Of course, in those days all the animals and the human beings lived together as one family, and all spoke the same language.

Maushop spoke to them all and said, "You all must have noticed how the family of Mother Earth is growing very quickly. That is because you have all been having babies, and your babies have grown up to have more babies, and they have grown to have more babies, so that as the generations go on, the world is starting to fill up. Just now there is plenty of room and enough food for everyone, but as we go on bringing more and more into the world and not sending anyone away, after a while there won't be enough room for everyone, and there won't be enough food. Plants will all be destroyed, animals will starve, and Mother Earth will suffer.

"Now, I can see two possible ways to solve this problem. In one of them you could just stop having babies and keep the same number as you have and just go on living in this way forever. In the other, if you want to keep bringing babies in through that door which you call Birth, then we should make another door, which we will call Death, and when you have been here for a while and experienced this world, then you would go through that other door and experience a different place."

Of course they all wanted to know about that other place, but Maushop said he hadn't been there and he didn't know much about it. He said that Matahdou was there waiting and had made a star path in the sky for them to follow down to the southwest. He said they would have to leave their bodies behind for Mother Earth to make into new life, because only their spirits could enter the land of souls. He said that it was an important decision that they would have to make for themselves, because whatever they decided, that's how it would be for all the generations to come.

So the animals and people all went into their clans, and the clans went into male and female groups, and each group began to council about what Maushop had said.

After a little while the men's groups were all finished, and when they came together they found they were all in agreement. They had all decided that they should stop having babies so that the world wouldn't get too full and they could all just go on living as they were forever. Then they looked around and saw that the women were coming out of their councils.

The female creatures had made one big circle, and so the men all went over and peeked into the circle to see what was going on. There in the center were all these little cubs—little lion cubs, wolf cubs, bear cubs, human-being cubs, all playing with one another, wrestling and biting one another's ears, and the women were all laughing and saying things like: "Oh, look at those two over there, aren't they cute!"

So the men all looked to the oldest clan chief and said, "Grandfather, speak for us."

So the oldest clan chief stepped out and said, "Well, the men creatures have had their meetings and we all agree. We all think it should be like this, that we will stop having babies so that the world won't fill up too much and we can just go on living as we are forever. Thank you."

There was silence for a moment, and everyone turned toward the oldest clan mother. So this grandmother stood up slowly and looked around at everyone and said, "Well, the women have had their meetings, too, and they have also come to an agreement. And that's not the way it's gonna be. We have decided that we want to go on having babies and bringing new little ones in through that door called Birth, and so we must have that other door called Death that we can go on through after a while. This is the reason we decided that: We have noticed that

we do not know enough yet about life and Creation here. Especially the human beings do not know enough. We keep making the same mistakes, and then we find new mistakes to make. But these little ones that come to us from the Creator, they are messengers. They bring us new teachings all the time from the Creator. They keep us on our toes so that we will do right for them, and not just for them, but for their children as well, and for all the unborn generations that are waiting to come here. When we understand that, then we must keep making a better world for them."

So, since it was the women who were in charge of birth and of raising those little ones, they were the ones who had the last word, and that's the way it has been ever since.

THE GREAT MIGRATION AND OLD MAN WINTER

At first the Children of the Morning Light lived on an island in a far southern sea. There it was warm all the time. Many fruits grew in the deep green forests below the mountain. Maushop taught them how to make his fishhooks, his fishing lines and nets, and the men fished all year in crystal turquoise waters. He taught them how to make spears and knives and what fruits to gather for food. The weather was warm all year, and life was rich and slow. The people were happy there. Perhaps life was too good, and they were getting lazy. Perhaps the people needed some trouble to stir themselves up a little.

One day Maushop came and said that harsh changes were coming. He said that their island would be destroyed in fire and that they must make many boats and escape to another land. So the people set to work making many dugout canoes from the huge trees of the deep forest.

The island began to tremble, and the people quickly got into the canoes and put to sea. When they were a little way off, the mountain roared and began to explode with fire and smoke. As they sailed away, the smoke stood up from the horizon and darkened the sky for days.

Eventually they came to a big land. When they landed, the people who lived in that place were afraid and angry and fought with them and forced them away. The Children of the Morning

Light fled high into the mountains that rose behind the coast. There they built a large village from the stones of the mountain.

After that they were often attacked by raiders who came with big war parties and looted and pillaged their village. So the people built a whole village underground, right under the other one. Then when the raiders came, they all just went down to the underground village and stayed until the raiders went away.

That worked well for many generations. But one time the raiders came and said, "Well, this is a nice village all built for us with nobody in it. Why don't we just stay and live here?"

For a while the people lived below the raiders without the raiders ever knowing they were there. Sometimes at night they would send a party up above to get things they needed. They never got caught, but the raiders wondered what happened to things they were missing. They decided it must be the little people, because they never saw them.

But the people got tired of living like that, never seeing the sun, and it seemed the raiders were not going to go away. So one night they all crept out of the underground village and left, very quietly, taking all they could with them down the mountains.

Then the Children of the Morning Light began a long migration north. On their travels they met many different people, and they stayed with some of them for a while. But the ways of the other people always seemed a little strange to them, so eventually they would begin to move once more, always heading north, following the fixed star around which all the others danced.

At one point the water began to rise around them. It seemed the tides of the sea were getting higher and never going out again. The people headed for higher ground, with the sea always at their feet behind them. Eventually they were on the peaks of the mountains, and there was no higher to go. They thought they would be drowned, because there were no trees up there to make dugout canoes from. They gathered around a fire and prayed to Kiehtan the Creator to send their old helper Maushop to save them. Maushop did not come at that time, but the rising waters slowed and then stopped.

The mountain peaks were like islands now, and some of the people were nervous that maybe the mountains might explode, as their stories had told them had happened to their old home so long ago. But they waited and kept praying and thanking Kiehtan for sparing them and for the beauty of the lands and the seas. Soon the waters began slowly to recede, and the land below lay hidden in a great white fog. They stayed together very close in their clans so that they would not lose anyone, and they went on down into the fog and kept moving north.

Pretty soon they saw that they were on ice and snow. As the fog cleared, they saw nothing but ice and snow everywhere. Some said they had gone too far north, so they turned toward the sun and went south. But the ice and snow continued. It went on and on and on, until the people thought that the whole world must be covered in ice and that they would never see a tree or the sea again.

The Children of the Morning Light prayed to Kiehtan again, and this time Maushop heard the prayer and came himself. He knew there must be something wrong, that it was not right for winter to stay so long over all the land. And so he went off in search of Paponny, or Pebon, as some call him, Old Man Winter.

Up in the north he found the lodge of Winter, a lodge made of ice. So Maushop called out to the old man.

"Paponny—are you there? Pebon, it's Maushop come to see you."

Now Old Man Winter didn't want to see Maushop because he knew Maushop would want to make him move away, but he had to be hospitable, for that is Kiehtan's instruction to us all, so he invited Maushop into his ice lodge.

"Sit down, Maushop," he said. "Have some cold tea and boiled bread and smoke a pipe with me."

So to be polite Maushop had some cold tea and boiled bread. But Paponny had put something in them, and when Maushop ate and drank and started to smoke the pipe, he got very sleepy.

Pebon just sat there boasting about how powerful he was.

"I'm so powerful that where I walk everything freezes and fills up with snow. I blow and the lakes and rivers all become hard and stiff. I pull all the leaves from the trees and load the branches down with ice. I…" But by that time Maushop was fast asleep, and Paponny went away.

After a long time Maushop woke and knew he had been tricked. Then he knew what he had to do. He started down the trail to the south and kept on going until he came to the place where the grass was growing and there were flowers and leaves on the trees and birds and insects singing everywhere. He went into a very old forest of tall trees, following the sound of a flute.

Deep in the forest was a clearing, and in the center was a big circle of Pugwudgies, the little people, all dancing around a beautiful young woman and a fine-looking young man who played the flute. Maushop told them all about old Paponny.

The woman, dressed in yellow buckskin and a green shawl, was called Nepon, or Summer. She said to the young man, who was dressed with ribbons of many colors and whose name was Sequan, or Spring, "Brother, talk to our elder brother. It seems he does not know when it is time to leave."

So Sequan set out for the north, playing his flute as he went. When he came to the snow, it melted around his moccasins wherever he stepped, and the grass began to grow green there. When he got to the ice lodge, Pebon asked him to come in and have some cold tea and boiled bread, but Sequan said, "No, thanks, I am fasting today."

Then Pebon began to boast again, saying that when he roared a blizzard came and covered everything, and when he blew, the rivers and lakes all froze, animals hid in their holes, and birds flew south. Sequan listened politely until Pebon had exhausted all his boasts, and then he began to talk.

"I know how powerful you are, brother. It is true that you bring the ice and snow to cover the land where you are. But this land has been covered too long now. That is why I have come, because, as you know, where I go your snow melts. When I play my flute, the birds return from the south and begin to sing together, the rivers start to flow again, and the lakes become unfrozen; the bears come from their caves, and other animals wake in their holes; the trees bud and leaf, and the flowers appear on the earth again."

While he was talking the ice lodge started to melt and drip all over them as they sat there. Pebon's frozen hair melted and dripped sadly down his face, and he began to be afraid that he might melt himself. So he said, "Enough—what do you want?"

Sequan told him that he must move away farther north and stay away for eight months, but then he could return for four months. So that was the agreement they made, and that is how it has been in those latitudes ever since.

With the coming of spring the people were able to move on again. Some of them thought that where they were was a good place to stay, but others said they wanted to find the rising sun. They thought that if they could get back to the ocean, they might find the land of Maushop and live with him again. So they kept on, but some stayed there, and along the journey others stopped off in different places, but others kept going. When they got to the sea some more stopped, but a few others said it was too cold there, and followed the shore south until they came to a land with many little bays and rivers, and a big sandy cape, and a lot of islands.

The people said, "This is the land where Maushop lives. We will stay here and be his people so that he may still be our teacher." And to this day our people live in the Pokonoket country of the deep saltwater bays, the big cape, and the islands of southeastern Massachusetts.

MORE TALES OF MAUSHOP

There are many tales of Maushop, who was a special helper to our people, the Wampanoag. Maushop was a helper of the Creator and it was he who, with his twin brother, Matahdou, helped to build the earth on the back of the great turtle and to make all the plants and animals we have. When human beings were created, Maushop became the helper and teacher of our people. And now I'll tell you some tales of Maushop after the Creation was finished.

MAUSHOP
AND GRANDFATHER SUN

This is the story of Maushop and Grandfather Sun.

There was a time long ago, in the morning of the world, when the sun went away and only showed up for a few minutes every day. At first our people didn't notice that the sun was going away because it all happened so gradually. One day there'd be a few minutes less of daylight, and the next there would be a few minutes less, and so on. And it kept on like this until people began to get worried.

"There's not enough time to plant our corn and beans and squash," they said. "We don't have enough light to hunt," they said. "There's only night fishing now, and the children can't go out and play because it's dark all the time, and they're getting bored and restless."

Everyone was getting restless because they had to sit inside the lodges and keep fires going all the time so that they could see. They were running out of firewood and running out of food. The children had heard all the stories there were, over and over, and sung all the songs there were, over and over, and played all the indoor games they knew, over and over. Everybody was restless and bored and hungry. They kept waiting for Grandfather Sun to come back. Now Grandfather Sun was coming for only about a minute; he had only just pulled all of himself out of the sea in the southeast when he dipped back down under the sea in the southwest.

"Something is certainly not right; it seems that Nepaushet Keesukwand, our grandfather, has abandoned us. We must talk to Maushop."

Now you know, Maushop was created helper, the one who had helped make all the plant people and the animal people and the human people and taught them all how to survive and live in harmony on the earth. He taught people how to find Grandfather Sun's power in the flint, the dry grass, the moss, and the wood, and how to make their fires from that. He taught them how to make spears and harden the points in the fire and how to hunt and fish with these. He taught them how to make knives and hatchets and arrows and spearheads and bowls and mortars out of stones. He taught them how to make their houses by cutting young trees and standing them in the ground, bending and tying them together and covering them with bark in winter and cattail rushes in summer. He taught them how to make their clothes and blankets and bowstrings and fish lines and fishnets from the skins of animals. He taught them how to make canoes by burning and scraping out the insides of big trees. Now the people again came to Maushop, as they did in those times when they were in trouble. After Maushop heard about the sun, he promised to speak to him as he rose from the sea the next morning.

When the first pale light began to dim the stars above the eastern sea, Maushop made himself tall as a giant and waded out into the ocean. In the southeast the sky went from dark blue to turquoise to pink to orange, and when the fiery tip of the sun poked up over the horizon, Maushop began to address him like this:

"O great Nepaushet Keesukwand, Grandfather Sun, the people have asked me to come and speak to you. They notice that you come now for only a few minutes every day, and the rest of the time they are in darkness, and they cannot hunt or grow their corn and beans and squash. They live on fish, which they catch by torchlight; they have little food and little firewood because fires burn all the time; the children cannot go out to play; and they are restless and bored and hungry." Well, that is what Maushop wanted to say, but before he could get all that out, Grandfather Sun had already slipped away into the hills of the southwest, and it was dark again.

Maushop waited through the long darkness, and when it grew light again in the southeast, he waded deep into the ocean, and when the first rays shot over the horizon, he began to speak very quickly.

"Grandfather, the people have asked me to speak to you because they notice you only come for a few minutes every day, and the rest of the time they cannot hunt or plant their beans and squash and corn, and they have little food or firewood, and everyone is bored and restless and hungry." But Grandfather Sun had disappeared again.

And the third time Maushop went to speak to Grandfather Sun, it was the same story. So Maushop took a lot of long, thin strands of seaweed and he wove them together into a huge net, the biggest net there ever was, a fishing net big enough to catch the sun. Maushop took the net and waded way out into the ocean, near the horizon where the sun appeared, and waited there up to his waist in the dark water, swinging his net slowly, while the stars wheeled above him.

When the sky grew light in the southeast, he got ready and began to whirl the great net around his head. Around and around and around and around he whirled the net. And then when the fiery head of the sun bobbed up from the horizon, he let the net loose, and it flew circling around and around till it fell right on top of the sun. The sun was completely caught in the net and began to struggle to get out. But Maushop grabbed the ends of the net and pulled them tight and held them so that there could be no escape. The harder the sun struggled, the harder Maushop pulled on the net and held him fast.

"Let me go. What's going on? What is this thing? What's— how did—what is this thing, anyway? *Let me go!*"

"Grandfather, I'm very sorry to have to do this, but you would not listen to me. I will let you go if you promise to hear me out."

"Oh, very well, I promise."

"All right, I'll let you out, but you must sit still now and listen."

"Yes, yes, I'll listen and just move along slowly so that I don't burn the sea and set it boiling. Now, what is it?"

And Maushop told Grandfather Sun all that the people had told him.

"That's very interesting," said Grandfather Sun. "I didn't even know those people cared. Nobody used to pay any attention to me when I used to spend a lot of time there. When I came in the morning, everyone was asleep. And I watched them all day, but no one ever looked up to talk to me, and at night no one ever came to say good-bye to me, or even ask me to come back. They all just ignored me. I thought they didn't like me. It's a lonely job that way, you know. But around on the other side of the world there are people who are very friendly and greet me every morning and smile at me all day and wave good-bye to me at night. So I began to spend more and more time there and less and less time over here. Now I just put in a quick appearance here because the Creator said I have to be here some every day."

"Well, Grandfather, you certainly have a good point there. I'll go and talk to the people and see what they have to say. Please don't go away again, and I'll be right back."

The people were glad to see the sun come back, but when Maushop told them what he had said, they all looked very sheepish and ashamed and kicked their toes in the dirt.

"What can we say? He's right."

"We haven't been very friendly at all."

"I guess we didn't realize that Grandfather Sun might have feelings."

"We certainly wouldn't like to be treated that way ourselves."

"What shall we do?"

So Maushop went back to Grandfather Sun and said, "The people are very ashamed and say they are very sorry. They're glad you told them what was wrong so that they can do something about it. They have decided that from now on they will wait in their doorways to greet you when you come, keep you company during the day, and come to say good-bye at sunset."

And from that time on, our people have taught their children to say, "Good morning, Grandfather Sun. It's good to see you again today. Thank you for coming back and giving us a good day in which to be alive and to learn." And in the middle of the day the people stop their work in the village and in the sea and look up and greet Grandfather sometimes: "Hello up there, Grandfather. It's good seeing you rolling around in the sky. Thank you for making us warm and for making everything so beautiful." And at the end of the day they stand on a hill and look at where the sun is going down in the west and say, "Good-bye, Grandfather. Thank you for this beautiful day. Have a good journey to that other side, but hurry on back tomorrow. We'll be waiting for you."

After that the sun never stayed away so long again. During part of the year he spends more time in that other part of the world, and our days here are shorter and the nights longer, but then he spends more time here to make up for that, and then we have longer days and shorter nights for our summer. During the times that the sun begins to go away or begins to come back, our people have ceremonies, and then we tell our children this story so that they will always know how important is Nepaushet Keesukwand, Grandfather Sun, bringer of all warmth and energy and the light of beauty.

MAUSHOP
AND THE PORPOISES

Now I want to tell you the story of Maushop and the porpoises. Of course the Children of the Morning Light are fishing people. We have always lived close to the sea, and our lives are tied to the water—to the lakes, the streams that flow from the lakes to the bays that fill with herring in early spring, the tides that fill the coves and race around the capes. Maushop taught our people how to make their canoes, how to make lines and hooks and spears, and how to make fishnets. He taught them how to make fish weirs, which are poles put down through the water into the ground with nets strung around them, so that fish will swim in and get caught. The people loved Maushop and always went to him for advice when they were in trouble.

Now you know that Maushop's twin brother, Matahdou, made all the things that are poisonous and dangerous on the earth. And when they were making the fish, Matahdou made a huge fish with long sharp teeth and little beady eyes and a nasty disposition. This fish began right away to attack all the creatures of the sea, and when it found the people's fish weirs, it tore them apart and had a feast on the fish inside. It didn't mind chewing on the fishermen, too, if any happened to be in the way.

The people tried talking to the fish, to try to make some agreement to share the fishing, but it just wouldn't listen. So then they went to Maushop and asked him if there wasn't something he could do about this terrible fish.

Maushop went down to the shore to talk to him.

"The people have sent me to council with you. They see that you are very hungry a lot, but they don't like it that you tear up their fish weirs and even tear up any people who may be in the water, too. They wonder if they might not make some agreement so that you could get enough to eat and leave them undisturbed."

Well, that's what Maushop tried to say, but before he could get very much of his speech out, that old fish just turned its back on him and began swimming out to sea, where it didn't have to listen. Every time that fish came around, Maushop tried to talk to it, but it always swam away.

Now you know when you are talking to people and they just turn their backs on you without listening, sometimes it makes you angry. It made Maushop so angry that he shouted at the fish.

"Hey, you! You—you come back—I haven't finished—hey!" But the fish just kept on swimming, and that got Maushop so angry that he threw his spear at the disappearing fish. The spear sailed through the air and stuck right on the top of the fish's back. But that old fish was so tough and mean it didn't even stop, but dived under the water. It managed to knock the handle off that spear by rolling it on the sand, but the blade stayed stuck fast in his back.

Well, you know that was a little help to the people, because at least they could see that fish coming by the blade that stuck up and cut through the waves as it swam into the bay.

Now Maushop went to the next-largest animals in the sea around there. They were the porpoises, which are a kind of dolphin. They were playing together when Maushop found them, because all dolphins like to play all the time. When I was a little boy and sailed my boat in the bay, the porpoises always came and played around my boat. They were great fun and good friends, and later I understood that they were also protecting and teaching me.

Maushop told the porpoises about the people's problem with this terrible fish and asked them to help, because they could swim as fast as that fish. But the porpoises were doubtful.

"You don't want to mess around with that fish. It doesn't listen to anybody. It's just plain mean."

"Vicious."

"Nasty."

"Have you seen the teeth on that guy?"

"We don't have any weapons like that; besides, we're nonviolent."

"Yeah. Peace and love, that's our thing."

"Yes," said Maushop, "but you do have one weapon that that fish doesn't have, and that makes all the difference."

"What's that?"

"Brains. You are very intelligent beings, and that fish just doesn't have any smarts at all. In fact, it's stupid! So I know you can figure it out."

Well, the porpoises formed a circle to have a council and put their minds together. They began to think out loud. It was a regular think tank.

"Well," the first one said, "what are we going to do about this big ugly old fish? Let's kick around some ideas."

The second one said, "Well, we can't fight, that's for sure. It would just tear us apart."

"I think we should come from our strength, do what we do best," said another.

"Well, what is our strength?" said the next one. "What do we do best?"

"That's easy," said another. "What we do best is have fun. We are experts in play."

"Just party animals, that's what we are."

"That's it! We'll play him to death!" shouted another. They all got excited.

"Yeah, we'll just keep playing with him no matter what he does."

"He'll either have to loosen up and join us, or we'll drive him crazy!"

"All right!"

"Great idea!"

Because, you see, they knew that whenever you can solve a problem, do something you have to do, and have fun doing it, you know you're doing right. In fact, if what I am doing isn't fun, I always stop and think about it, because probably I'm either going about it wrong, or it's not a good thing to be doing. That's why we were given the gift of joy, the old ones tell us, to guide us on the right path.

So the next time that big fish came slipping down into the bay looking for fish weirs, there came the porpoises! They came diving and rolling and splashing and whistling and laughing.

That mean old fish rolled its beady little eyes up at them, "Get away from me! I don't have time for your nonsense now! I'm busy! Go away and play! Idiots!"

Then the porpoises made a big circle around the fish and started singing and bringing the circle in closer and closer to it, keeping it from going where it wanted to go.

"Whatsamatter, you deaf? I don't want to play. Get out of here, you clowns! Take your silly games somewhere else! I don't want any of your craziness now!"

But now the porpoises began to run at the fish, swimming very fast and jumping over it, landing *splash* right by its head and running under it so that the points of their dorsal fins would run along its belly and tickle it. "Wooo, eeee—*stop that, you—ooo eeee!*"

And then some porpoises began to race at it and butt it in its sides with their heads, and some bit its tail and jerked it backward. It was pulled this way and butted that way and tickled and spun around until it was dizzy.

Finally that big mean ugly old fish couldn't stand any more and it turned and swam as fast as it could for the deepest, farthest part of the sea. And all the people who were on the shore watching let out a great cheer for the victory of the porpoises.

The porpoises must have told the other dolphins the story, because if you go down to the ocean even now and you see the porpoises or any dolphins playing there, you know it will be perfectly safe to go into the water. To this day there's not a shark that will hang out when the dolphins are playing, because they will still drive it crazy. And that's the truth!

CHEEPII KEEPS HIMSELF SAFE

Do you remember Hobomoko? You remember he was the spirit helper, the starmaker who sang up the fire of Grandfather Sun? And he was the one who always thought there was something wrong with everything, that the Creator didn't do a good job, that there were mistakes and bad, evil things in the Creation. He was always complaining, but the other spirit helpers never paid attention because that was not how they thought.

One day this Hobomoko was down around our people, looking for someone to talk to, and he saw a man by the name of Cheepii sitting by himself and working on making fishnets. So Hobomoko came along and started to tell him about how the creation was a big mistake and the Creator didn't make things right; about how it was a pretty shaky thing and liable to come apart anytime; and about how there were dark, evil, mysterious things in it that were eager to take control and destroy it all.

Well, Cheepii was really amazed to hear all that. He wondered if it could be true. But if it was, why hadn't he ever heard anything like that before? On the other hand, if the Creation was really perfect, and the Creator hadn't made any mistakes, then why had the Creator made something like Hobomoko who was going around saying it was all wrong?

Cheepii began to think there might be something in what

Hobomoko was saying, so he said, "Well, if that's true, what can we do?"

"If I were you," Hobomoko told him, "I would try to protect myself. I would try to find all the magic I could and surround myself with spells to protect me when the dark times come and everything starts coming apart."

So Cheepii began to learn and collect magic. He went to every magician he could find to collect magic, and then he began to gather it on his own. He found power objects—magic stones, roots, teeth and claws and feathers from magic creatures—and he began spending more and more time doing that, and doing rituals burning special herbs, drinking special potions. He began to neglect his garden and his canoe and his house.

People were curious why he was doing all this, but he only said, "Don't bother me now. It's a very dangerous situation. I have no time to talk."

Pretty soon the others began to say, "I think that's just a lot of silly superstition, but you never know. What if he's right? Maybe we should do a little of that magic, too, just to be safe."

They got so worried and thought so much about the dangers and the evils that lurked in the shadows of the world that it made them sick, and they started going to Maushop to be cured.

When Maushop saw that all these people were getting sick, he knew something was up, and when he found out what they were doing, he gathered everyone together for a big healing ceremony. When he got them all in the circle, he spoke to them.

"The reason all you people have been getting sick is

because you believe there is something evil and wrong in Creation. You think the Creator has made mistakes and can't help you. When you start to worry all the time about what might go wrong, you make yourselves sick.

"Now the fact is, there is nothing at all wrong with this Creation. The Creator hasn't made any mistakes, and everything works just right. Of course, every kind of idea has to be available in this Creation, so I guess somebody has to believe the way Hobomoko does, and people like Cheepii and you are free to believe it, too, if you choose.

"But it doesn't seem as though all this magic is doing you any good. You are just getting sicker all the time. Now if you come back and follow the ways of the Creator, the original instructions, you will be all right. Those original instructions are just the laws of nature, the way things work, and there are three ways that you can learn about them.

"First of all, you can observe the operation of nature. That is the way of science. You can see that the Creator gave the geese instructions to fly south before the winter, but crows and blue jays have different instructions. You can see that the strawberries come early and the grapes come late. You can watch the seasons and see how the other creatures survive.

"Second, you can seek the truth of Creation inside yourself. For the Creator is in you, too. That is the way of meditation. Alone on a hill, in a vision pit or a sweat lodge, in dreams, the Creator will sing in your heart and whisper in your ear and set your feet upon the path of beauty.

"The third way is in the accumulated knowledge of the people from ancient times until today. This is the way of tradition. In our ceremonies the stories and songs and lore of the people are passed on from generation to generation.

"So by observing nature, by listening to Creation's song within your own heart, and by learning the wisdom of the people as transmitted by the elders, you will know the ways of the Creator, and you will be all right.

"Remember you were born perfect into a perfect universe—the Creator didn't make any mistakes. This is how you and all your generations to come can live in harmony always, in the natural joy and beauty of Creation."

So the people put away all that magic and they started to get well again and to live in a good way. All except Cheepii. He was upset that no one believed him anymore, and he ran around making mischief and causing trouble for a while. We have stories about that, too.

But at last he gave up and went away. We think he must have gone off trying to find other people to convince about Hobomoko's teachings.

We never saw him again, but some think he must have found other people who believed him, because about four hundred years ago a lot of boat people started landing on our shores, all dressed in black and talking about evil and sin and damnation and the devil!

MUCKACHUCK

The last story of Maushop I'll tell
is the story of Muckachuck.

Now after Maushop had made the world safe for the people, after he had beaten all the monsters and the giants and the wicked sorcerers, he began to realize that the people were starting to come to him for help for every little thing that they should have been able to do for themselves.

He understood that as long as he was around, they would tend to rely on him and never become strong and independent people.

So he had a big farewell feast and told them all he was going away to the east, beyond the rising sun, and that from then on they would have to learn to take care of themselves.

When he was getting ready to go, someone came to him and said, "Well, I guess it's a good thing you are going now before you have met the last great sorcerer, because his magic is too powerful for you."

Maushop was surprised, and then he said, "There's no sorcerer who has greater magic than I have. Who is this magician?"

"His name is Muckachuck, and he is much more powerful than you are, so it is good you never met him."

It is too bad, but I must be truthful and tell you that this hit Maushop in his pride, and he began to get just a little bit angry.

"Where is this Muckachuck? I'll meet him right now and settle this before I go."

"Well, he lives in a lodge out on Wachusett Mountain."

Maushop went quickly and found that lodge, and he called out, "Muckachuck, are you in there? This is Maushop. Come out; I want to talk to you."

From inside the lodge there was a sound like, "Goo, goo, gee-goo."

"Muckachuck, I didn't understand that. Are you inviting me to come in?"

"Goo, goo, gee-gee, goo."

"Muckachuck, if you don't come out, I'm going to understand you are inviting me to come in."

"Goo, gee, gee, goo."

"All right, here I come."

Inside the lodge there was nothing except a little baby sitting on the ground in the very middle. He was so little that he couldn't walk yet, but he was sitting up and saying, "Goo, goo, gee, goo."

"Ho, ho, Muckachuck, that's a very clever disguise, but you don't fool me. Let me show you some real magic now. What do you think of this?"

And Maushop changed himself into a big mountain lion and roared at the baby. But instead of being frightened, the baby went, "Goo, gee, goo, goo," and tried to pull the lion's ears and hug it.

Maushop was a little irritated that he hadn't impressed

Muckachuck, so he quickly changed himself into a snake and came slithering up as though he were going to bite, but the baby just laughed and wanted to play with the snake and hug it, too.

Now Maushop was getting really annoyed, "You like snakes? Well, let's see how you like this."

And he changed himself into a huge eagle and flew at the baby to tear at him with great sharp claws, but the baby laughed and wanted to pull at its feathers and hug it.

"All right, Muckachuck. Now I'm getting angry. You won't like this so much."

And Maushop changed himself into a ring of fire all around the baby, with the flames closing in and getting hotter. The baby didn't think that was so cute and he began to go, "Uh, uh, wa." And then he hollered, "Wa, wa, waaa, waaaaaa! *Waaaaa!*"

The baby's tears splashed on the fire, and suddenly Maushop felt very sorry. He changed himself back into his own form and tried to comfort the baby.

"There, there, baby! It's all right. I didn't mean to frighten you. See, it's just me again. Come on, let's play. Don't cry anymore—look, look at this."

And Maushop took off his medicine bag from around his neck and dangled it in front of the baby to get his attention and amuse him.

The baby looked at it, stopped crying, and grabbed the medicine bag out of Maushop's hand.

"Goo, goo, gee, goo!"

"Oho, Muckachuck, that was pretty clever! Now you have my medicine bag. I see that what they say about you is true— you are a very powerful sorcerer, indeed! I guess I'll let you win

this one. Keep the medicine bag—it's my gift to a mighty magician. But you didn't harm me, and you seem like a pretty good little fellow, so what if I just go on my way as though this never happened? I won't say anything about it if you don't. Use my medicine bag to help the people. *Wuniish*—go in beauty."

And Maushop went away to the east and has never come back, although perhaps if things get bad enough, he might.

And Muckachuck—well, Muckachuck means "little fellow" in our language. Muckachuck is the spirit of little ones, the spirit of children everywhere, and we say that it is the most powerful spirit there is.

And we say that whenever you go into a room and there's a baby there all by himself and he is just laughing for no reason at all and going, "Goo, goo, gee, goo," well, we say that he is singing his war song, and he is remembering the time when he beat Maushop.

Now you have heard some of our Song of Creation and tales of Maushop, and about the journeys of our people to come to where they are.

The Old Storyteller stirs up the coals again. The soft light dances in his eyes, and he seems to see through many ages of time. After a moment of thought, listening to the quiet hiss of the fire, he speaks once more.

These are more than stories, you know. They are the heart of our culture. You ask if they are true. They are as true as anything in the world. For they are who we are, our memories and our dreams. And even if all our lands and everything are taken from us, if we have our stories we still survive. We know who we are and where we have been, and we are a people, the People of the Dawn, the Wampanoag, Children of the Morning Light.